Brookie's Adventure

by Jean Bell

CONSCIOUS
KIDS NETWORK

Published by Conscious Kids Network

Dedication

To my beloveds—Brooklynn, Chike, Sarah-Jean, and Simone.

AcknowLedgments

I want to thank Vicky Paz and Lakia Ross for their amazing, joyful illustrations and
Ty Andrews for his creative vision and direction.
You have a place eternally in my heart!

Brookie wakes up bright and early and begins to think about what the kids at school said about God yesterday. Brookie jumps out of bed and heads to her sister Sarah's room. Brookie takes her sister's sleepy face into her hands and tells her to wake up.

"Brookie, it's Saturday! Why are you up so early?"

"Sarah, all the kids at school say they found God. Some of them say they found Jesus, and Jesus is God. I told them that Jesus Rodriquez is not God, he's our dentist, and they gave me a strange look. Anyway, do I have to find God, and if so, where should I look?"

"Brookie, what are you talking about? God isn't missing! Go ask Mom."

Brookie opens Sarah's eyes with her fingers and says, "You have to focus, this is important! All the kids at school have different gods. I think one is named Jehobah, one's named Ahlen, and one I think is Vishwho. Oh, and one is named Holy Jeezus! And all this time, I thought there was only one God. Where did these other gods come from, and do I have to find all of them or just one?"

Sarah looks at her sister with one eye open and says, "That is not how you pronounce their names! The correct way to pronounce their names is Jehovah, Allah, Vishnu, and Jesus. And no, you don't have to find any of them! Now go away and let me sleep!"

"Well, you're no help, sleepy head!" And with a bounce off the bed, Brookie dashes out of her sister's room, brushes her teeth, washes her face, gets dressed, and heads downstairs to breakfast.

Brookie, while deep in thought, plays with her toast. Her mother notices and says, "Is there something wrong with the toast, darling?"

"Mom, the kids at school all say they found God, and I'm not sure where to look for God, and is God a man or a woman? All the kids refer to God as He."

Her mother is amazed at Brookie's questions, and says, "Well, dear, God doesn't have a gender. Brookie, where do you think God is?"

"I don't know, maybe at our church. The kids at school say God lives in the sky in a place called Heaven just behind the moon. Some say God lives in nature. I just don't know." Suddenly, Brookie pops up out of her seat and declares, "But I'm going to find out."

Her mother is about to tell her that God is Spirit and is a part of her and a part of all life, but before she can say a word, Brookie runs out the door and says, "I'm headed to the meadow to find God!"

Brookie's mother gives her husband a worried look, and he says, "She'll be all right. I will check on her a little later."

Brookie skips and bounces through the meadows with her dog, Mr. Bangles, and comes across a big, round bumblebee flying low and slow! "Hello, bumblebee," she says.

To Brookie's surprise, the bumblebee turns and, in a sing-song buzzy kind of way, says, "Bzzz, greetings, little girl and dog."

Brookie blinks her eyes several times, and with her mouth ajar, she stares in disbelief that a bee just spoke to her.

Brookie manages to close her mouth and says, "How are you able to talk? You're just a bee!" The bee looks at Brookie with a frown and proclaims, "Bzzz, just a bee? Bzzz, just a BEE! How are you able to talk? You're just a GIRL. Bzzz!" The bee huffs and begins to slowly fly away.

12

"Wait, wait, don't go! I'm sorry I upset you," Brookie yells after the bee. "Let me start over. My name is Brookie and this is Mr. Bangles."

Mr. Bangles lets out an approving bark toward the bee. The bee is still upset but decides to stay since it's not every day he has a chance to talk to a little girl.

"Bzzz, my name is Buzz Bumblebee! What brings you to my meadow?"

"Your meadow!" Brookie belts out before she realizes it. "My parents bought this meadow and farm last year," Brookie tells the bee.

Buzz proudly says, "My family has lived in this meadow since, bzzz, since, bzzz, well, forever. So they're our meadows!"

Brookie notices that Buzz was getting upset again and asks, "Where does your family live?"

"Bzzz, that's top secret because everybody wants our bee-licious honey!"

"Oh, I see," Brookie says with a smile.

"What brings you to my meadow today, little Brookie girl?"

With a sad tone, Brookie says, "I'm looking for God, and I don't know where to start. I was hoping to find someone who could point me in the right direction."

Buzz becomes so excited he begins to fly around in circles and shrieks, "Bzzz, I know, I know where God is! Come this way, come this way and I will show you!"

Brookie and Mr. Bangles charge up the hill after Buzz Bumblebee, who is flying faster than any bee Brookie has ever seen.

When they reach the top of the hill, Brookie freezes in amazement and delight! Down the other side of the hill are thousands—no, millions—of beautiful purple, red, orange, and yellow wildflowers!

Buzz flies in front of Brookie's face and says, "Bzzz, see how bee-utiful God is! And God returns every spring and provides us with bee-lightful nectar to nourish us!"

Buzz begins to weave through the flowers with joy and love. Brookie is so in awe of the colorful flowers, she and Mr. Bangles begin to run through them, laughing and carefree! As she reaches the bottom of the hill, she rolls into a patch of grass and giggles with delight.

Buzz Bumblebee flies by and says, "See, little Brookie girl, isn't God bee-utiful?"

"Oh yes, Mr. Buzz, very beautiful!"

Brookie didn't tell Buzz that the field of flowers is not her idea of where God lives; besides, he's too excited to listen anyway.

"I must go to work now, little Brookie girl. Bee good and come visit me any time in my meadow!"

"I will, Mr. Buzz Bumblebee, and thank you!" Buzz bops, buzzes, and flies away into the field of wildflowers. Brookie turns to Mr. Bangles and anxiously says, "We have to find God before dinner."

Mr. Bangles licks Brookie on her cheek, and she giggles.

"Excuse me!
Excuse me, but maybe I can help—would love to help!"

Brookie looks around but doesn't see anyone. "Who's there?" Brookie yells, "Come out and show yourself!"
Out pops a long-eared gray bunny rabbit from behind a nearby tree. Brookie is astounded at all the talking creatures she's encountering today—first a bee and now a rabbit!

"Hello, hello, my name is Sarah. What's your name?"

"Sarah," Brookie chirps, "that's my sister's name!"

Sarah Rabbit becomes upset at the thought that someone else has her name and says, "Oh no, oh no, it's my name, and your sister can't have it! She must give it back, must give it back to Sarah!"

Sarah the bunny hops around frantically with a worried frown on her face.

Brookie wants to laugh but composes herself and tells the rabbit, "Don't worry, Sarah, more than one person...umm...and bunny can be named the same thing."

Sarah Rabbit looks unsure and says, "Really, really, this is okay? I hope this is okay?"

Brookie smiles and says, "Yes, it is perfectly okay. My name is Brookie and this is Mr. Bangles."

"Oh, pleased to meet you, so pleased to meet you," Sarah exclaims as she hops closer to the two. Mr. Bangles runs and hides behind Brookie, not sure what to think about a talking rabbit.

"Come out, come out, Mr. Bangles!" Sarah coos at Mr. Bangles, but he stays put for now.

Brookie excitedly says, "So you can help me find God?"

"Oh, definitely, definitely, and it is a magnificent, wonderful place where God is! A really big place—a majestic place! Come with me and I will show you!"

Brookie and Mr. Bangles follow Sarah Rabbit along a lovely trail beside a crystal-clear creek. Brookie marvels at the beautiful landscape and is glad her parents decided to move here.

Soon the three are standing in front of a tall, wide apple tree with branches filled with rich, green leaves and big, red apples. At the base of the tree, the roots separate and create an inverted V-shaped area big enough for a rabbit to create a burrow.

To Brookie's amazement, Sarah taps her foot five times and out of the burrow climb ten little bunny rabbits and Papa Rabbit! They all run over to Brookie and greet her with lots of nose rubs. Brookie kneels down to greet the bunnies, and she tips over onto the ground. In a twinkle of an eye, Brookie and Mr. Bangles are covered in bunny rabbits! Brookie giggles and laughs as the little bunnies crawl all over her and tickle her with their whiskers. Even Mr. Bangles enjoys the affection from the little cottontail creatures. "Okay! Okay! Hi, nice to meet you! Okay, let me up already!" giggles Brookie as she tries to stand up. Sarah hops over and shoos her children to the side.

Sarah affectionately says to her family, "Look, I have new friends, new friends! This is little Brookie and Mr. Bangles! See, Brookie, isn't God glorious!" Sarah proclaims with outstretched arms toward the tree.

"God provides us with shelter at the tree's base and delicious apples in the warm time of the year. There are other parts of God very nearby that give us nuts for the cold time of the year." Sarah hops up and down and then turns to Brookie and declares, "See how grand God is, Brookie. God is right here as the apple tree, over there as the flowers in the fields, and everywhere for us!"

Brookie gazes upon the tall and majestic apple tree and follows the sun's rays as it streams through the branches and gently settles on the leaves. Brookie is speechless and takes in all the loveliness before her.

"Brookie? Brookie? Hello, little girl!" Sarah jumps up and waves her paws in front of Brookie's face.

Brookie snaps out of the stare, looks at Sarah, and says, "Yes, I'm here, and you're right, this tree is magnificent!"

Sarah smiles and says, "But it's not where you think God is?"

"I'm not sure anymore because now I am beginning to see why you and Buzz Bumblebee see God in the wildflowers and in this marvelous tree!"

Sarah smiles and whispers softly, "Brookie, you are a smart little girl! God is in ALL!" Brookie is confused by what Sarah Rabbit just said. She starts to ask her to explain what she means by "God is in ALL," but before she can say a word, Sarah hops up in Brookie's arms, kisses her cheek, hops down, and bids Brookie farewell.

"Wait, wait, I want to ask you something!" Brookie yells after Sarah as she and her family hop down the rabbit hole. Sarah, being last in line, turns and says, "Brookie girl, you will find your answers today; I know, I know you will. Follow your heart and come visit us soon!" And with a turn, Sarah is gone.

It's getting late, so Brookie decides to head home. As she walks along the creek, she marvels at how her day has unfolded. First, she met a talking bee and then a rabbit— nobody is going to believe her.

The sun glistens like diamonds on the water's surface, and Brookie decides to put her feet in the cool, refreshing water. As her feet dangle in the creek, a fish pops up and says, "Hello."

Brookie, startled by the sudden appearance of the fish, pulls her feet out of the water and lets out a loud gasp. Even after encountering a talking bee and rabbit, Brookie is still in awe of a fish greeting her. "Hello," Brookie says with caution.

"Hi, my name is Bruno Trout, and I'm sorry if I startled you. What's your name?" At this point, Brookie doesn't know what to think about this day, as weird and fantastic as it has been.

"My name is Brookie and this is Mr. Bangles." Brookie looks over at Mr. Bangles and wonders if he will start talking as well, but Mr. Bangles just barks at the fish.

"What brings you to my creek today?" Bruno happily asks.

"Well, my goodness, I've talked to a bee and a rabbit today. Why not talk to a fish! Mr. Bruno, my day started off with me trying to find God because everybody at school said they have found God, and I want to find God too. I met a bee and a rabbit, and they showed me where and what God is to them. Now, I'm not sure if God is really in any particular place to be found. None of the kids at school could show me where God is or even give me an address. My big sister can drive now, so if I had God's address, she could drive me there and we could meet God."

Bruno excuses himself and ducks under water. He comes up a few seconds later and says, "Fascinating! Do you have any idea about where God might be?"

"Not really, but when I was younger, I remember always being happy and warm. It was like being wrapped in love and joy! I figured such a wonderful feeling must be God! I remember Grandma once said God is love, I thought the happiness I felt must be God wrapped all around me."

Bruno looks at Brookie for a long time, and asks, "So where do you think God lives?"

"I don't know. Most of the kids at school say God lives in Heaven, and Heaven is in the sky, and God is an old man with a beard. Mom told me that God is Spirit and is not a man or a woman and that God is the life of us all. So I'm confused about where God is, what God is, and why all the kids think God has to be found. I think Mom is right about God living in us, but I'm just a little girl and I'm having a hard time understanding all of this. I want to find God before dinner, but I don't think that's going to happen."

"Well, little Brookie girl, God doesn't have to be found, and your mother is right. God is the life of all! And God is all around us in every living thing."

"So why do the kids at school say they've found God and God lives in Heaven far away?"

"Brookie, children usually learn about God from their parents, and some people believe that God is outside of themselves in a faraway place. Just remember that you can't find something you never lost in the first place. God is love and God is life. The energy we call life is God in us. So every living thing has the life of God in it! Everything is energy; everything is God. God is in ALL!"

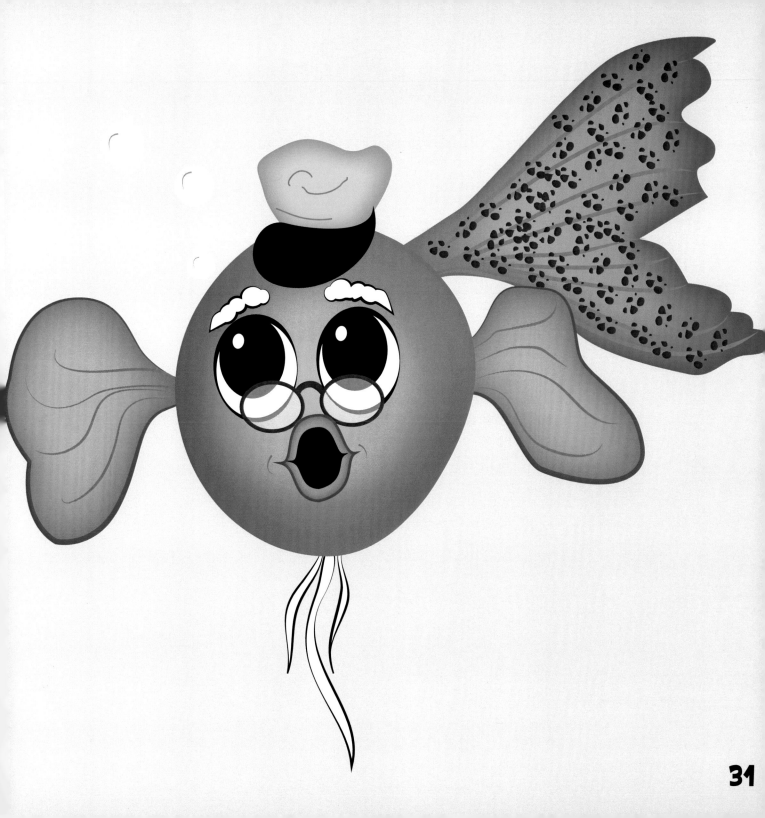

"So what you're saying is God is life and the life that is in everybody and every living thing is God?"

"Yes, you got it! And it's just as simple as that!"

"Wow, now I understand why Buzz Bumblebee and Sarah Rabbit thought God is the wildflowers and the apple tree! The flowers and the tree are a part of God! It's a lot to understand, but I think I got it. God is my life and the life of all that lives! I'm so glad I can stop looking for God now because I'm pooped."

Bruno Trout laughs. "Children are naturally filled with goodness and love, and God is natural goodness, so you're already on the right track. All you have to do is remember that God is within you and you can always connect with God by walking in nature, sitting silently, or by expressing happiness and joy through play, art, song, and dance."

"That's all I have to do? Just be a child and be happy and joyful, and I will connect with God? That sounds too good to be true! What's the catch?"

As Brookie lies down in the grass, Bruno explains that there is no catch and all she has to do is love life and be a happy child. Brookie's eyes become heavy with sleep. Mr. Bangles is sleepy too and curls up next to Brookie, and they both fall fast asleep as Bruno talks on and on and on.

"Brookie, Brookie darling, it's time to get up."

"Please, Mr. Bruno Trout, tell me more."

"Bruno Trout? Darling, wake up. It's your mother and it's time for breakfast!"

"Huh?" Brookie sits up and sees that she's in her room and says to her mother, "How did I get back home and in bed?"

Brookie's mother looks at her daughter a little strangely and says, "Darling, you went to bed last night on your own because you were tired from swimming in the creek with your sister all day. Come on, go wash up and get dressed because we are all going for a walk after breakfast."

"But I already went for a walk and I met Buzz Bumblebee, Sarah Rabbit and her family, and Bruno Trout! They all helped me find God, but I don't have to find God, because God is within me and all I have to do is remember that."

Brookie's mother smiles and says, "Yes, darling, you are absolutely right about God being within you! The bee, bunny, and fish you mentioned must have been a dream dear. Now hurry and get ready so we can eat and go for our walk!"

"So I was dreaming that Buzz Bumblebee, Sarah Rabbit, and Bruno Trout could talk? But it was so real, Mr. Bangles!"

At breakfast, Brookie tells her family all about Buzz Bumblebee, Sarah Rabbit, and Bruno Trout, and that she now knows that God is Spirit and is the life of all living things. Her family is fascinated with Brookie's story and her new understanding of God.

After breakfast, the entire family heads out for a lovely Sunday morning walk through the meadow by the creek. As they pass by the creek, Brookie sees Bruno Trout pop his head out of the water, and he stares at her with a slight smile on his face. Brookie can hardly believe her eyes and begins to yell, "Look, everybody, it's Bruno Trout! It's the wise old fish I told you about at breakfast!"

As the family turns to look in the creek, they see a fish swim away.

Brookie's father says, "That was a fine looking fish, Brookie; we should come here to fish one day!"

Brookie gives her father a look of total disgust and thinks there is no way she can eat Bruno Trout.

"No thanks, Dad! I think I'm sticking to veggies for a while!"

As they continue on their walk, they come upon the beautiful old apple tree, and there is an inverted V at the base of the tree, just like in Brookie's dream.

The family picks apples off the tree, and her mother says, "I'm going to make an apple pie for us this afternoon."

As the family gathers up the apples, Brookie sticks her head in the inverted V at the base of the tree, and there is a hole in the ground! A rabbit hole! Brookie says in a whisper, "Sarah, Sarah, are you down there?"

Brookie's sister Sarah sneaks up behind her and says, "No, silly, I'm right here!" Sarah picks up her little sister and twirls her around in the air, and they both giggle with delight. Everyone in the family has an armful of apples. Brookie makes sure the apple tree still has plenty of apples left for the rabbits, just in case they are real and not a dream.

As they begin to head home, Brookie turns to take one last look at the tree. To her surprise, she sees Sarah Rabbit and Buzz Bumblebee peeping out from behind the tree and waving at her. Just as Brookie is about to say something to her family, Sarah Rabbit holds up her paw to her mouth as if to say "keep us your secret." Sarah winks at Brookie and hops down the hole. Buzz Bumblebee flies by Brookie and gives her a knowing wink, then slowly bops away. Brookie's heart is filled with love and delight. She looks down at Mr. Bangles who lets out a loving bark, and then they both run and skip the rest of the way home.

About the Author

Jean Bell is a New Thought motivator and spiritual practitioner from Stone Mountain, Georgia. Jean is the co-founder of Conscious Kids Network and is devoted to creating metaphysical and fun-filled media entertainment for youths of all ages.